Acting Edition

I0741580

To Tell a Story About the Earth

by Miranda Rose Hall

No one shall make any changes in this title(s) for the purpose of production. No part of this book may be reproduced, stored in a retrieval system, scanned, uploaded, or transmitted in any form, by any means, now known or yet to be invented, including mechanical, electronic, digital, photocopying, recording, videotaping, or otherwise, without the prior written permission of the publisher. No one shall share this title(s), or any part of this title(s), through any social media or file hosting websites.

For all inquiries regarding motion picture, television, online/digital and other media rights, please contact Concord Theatricals Corp.

MUSIC AND THIRD-PARTY MATERIALS USE NOTE

Licensees are solely responsible for obtaining formal written permission from copyright owners to use copyrighted music and/or other copyrighted third-party materials (e.g. artworks, logos) in the performance of this play and are strongly cautioned to do so. If no such permission is obtained by the licensee, then the licensee must use only original music and materials that the licensee owns and controls. Licensees are solely responsible and liable for clearances of all third-party copyrighted materials, including without limitation music, and shall indemnify the copyright owners of the play(s) and their licensing agent, Concord Theatricals Corp., against any costs, expenses, losses and liabilities arising from the use of such copyrighted third-party materials by licensees. For music, please contact the appropriate music licensing authority in your territory for the rights to any incidental music.

IMPORTANT BILLING AND CREDIT REQUIREMENTS

If you have obtained performance rights to this title, please refer to your licensing agreement for important billing and credit requirements.

TO TELL A STORY ABOUT THE EARTH was commissioned by Concord Theatricals and developed by LubDub Theatre Co (Caitlin Nasema Cassidy and Geoff Kanick, Co-Artistic Directors; Miranda Rose Hall, Founding Playwright; Robert Duffley, Founding Dramaturg). The play received a developmental workshop at Georgetown University's Theater & Performance Studies Program in the Department of Performing Arts in October 2024. The Faculty Host was Professor Maya E. Roth. The production was co-directed by Caitlin Nasema Cassidy and Geoff Kanick with dramaturgy by Robert Duffley. The cast and creatives were as follows:

STUDENT COMPANY . . . . .Sophia Alexandrou, Daisy Casemore,
Tai Remus Elliot, Winnie Ho, Anna Kummelstedt,
Gabriela Martinez, Martin Neisuler, Julia Toloczko,
Nelly Amairany Hernández Valdez,
Alex Wang, Heran Zhang

Special Thanks

Dr. Peter P. Marra and the Earth Commons, Georgetown University's Institute for Environment & Sustainability

TO TELL A STORY ABOUT THE EARTH was subsequently produced by Franklin Performing Arts Company (Raye Lynn Mercer, Executive/Artistic Director) in February 2025. The produciton was directed by Eliza Palter. The cast and creatives were as follows:

COMPANY . . . . Heather Cohen, Aiden Day, Aida DiChiara,
Mike Hulbig, Liam Nolan-Hayun, Debra Packard,
Nathaniel Packard, Matthew Packard, Nick Paone,
Kylie Parsons, Catherine Rhodes, Kellie Stamp

CHARACTERS

THE LIBRARIAN – A Librarian, a generation or two above the others

TAYLOR – A Leader

JO – A Skeptic

SAM – A Visionary

CJ – A Romantic

RILEY – A Wise Fool

DEVISING CHORUS – An optional chorus, as big or small as you please, that helps with the creation and performance of an original ten-minute play

SETTING

A rehearsal space.

TIME

The ever-present now.

AUTHOR'S NOTES

A note on casting

When casting this play, think of these characters as archetypes. The roles are open in terms of race, gender, and other identities.

Some notes about this play

This is a play about devising. It's about what happens when a small ensemble tries to make a play from scratch. I think of it as a fairly traditional play that I have written in a fairly traditional way, but with one big twist: it's also a MadLib! There are prompts throughout the script for you to fill in as you see fit (but don't feel that you have to limit your writing based off of the size of the blank provided. If you have more to say – say it!) That means that the play will be different every time it's produced. My hope is that these blanks help the play be of you and of the place where you perform it in a more personal and immediate way than I could ever write on my own.

I come from a devising tradition with my own small theater company, LubDub Theatre Co. We have developed this play together, modeled after our own practices of devising and making work within climate crisis. We have found that talking about climate crisis is a very personal matter, and that talking about the entire Earth gets very overwhelming very quickly. The arc of this play reflects the arc that we have experienced creatively over the past five years: what is personal is emotionally resonant; what is emotionally resonant makes for good theater; and we need good theater to help us make sense of our rapidly-changing world.

And why do I think we need theater to help us make sense of our rapidly changing world? Because theater is made in community and shared in community. And community is our best defense against the anxieties, grief, and emergencies of our times.

In the sections that are yours to write, don't feel that you need to imitate my voice. I recommend experimenting with what these characters would say, workshopping things as a company, codifying a final draft, memorizing it, and then delivering it as if it were spontaneous material. Remember: the audience probably won't know that you're filling in blanks unless you tell them.

The biggest blank to fill in is the ten-minute play that you will create about a Subject of your choosing. Find a part of the natural world that everyone in your ensemble has a personal story about, and let that be your guide. These stories, and this Subject can be fairly simple, and even fairly ordinary. I have found that simplicity ultimately makes things all the more profound. (And if you'd like some guidance on a developmental process for all of this, please refer to the Note on Process in the Appendix of this Acting Edition.)

At the end of the day, what I care about the most is that each collaborator on this project might bring something of themselves that is specific, energizing, and personally meaningful. It is my assignment to you: bring something to life that you care about.

And I acknowledge that making something you care about may involve some emotional vulnerability. I hope that you may build a trusting and courageous space for all of the people making the play. It is a story about people who learn to hold each other. I hope that becomes true for your process as well.

And most importantly, please enjoy yourselves. It's called a play for a reason.

Scene One
The Pitch

*(**THE LIBRARIAN** makes a phone call.)*

(There need not be a literal phone, or any business of dialing.)

THE LIBRARIAN. Hi.

This is the Librarian.

I'm just coming out of your show!

I'm standing in the parking lot.

I didn't want to interrupt your celebration. You must be having a party!

But I couldn't wait another moment.

I'm calling with a proposition.

I'm making an offer you can't refuse.

The library is having an event next month, and there's a theme: Earth.

We have some things planned.

But something is missing.

And you know what that something is?

Performance.

And as I watched your show this evening, I thought: these people make theater.

They should make something for us!

And what should you make?

Well I think that you should just try...to...tell a story about the Earth.

(A beat.)

Now, people think that librarians are all about rules!

We're not!

But that being said, there are some guidelines.

I'm afraid that we cannot have any of the following:

bad language, adult themes, excessively loud sound cues, fireworks, animals, literal fires or literal floods –

And let's keep it under ten minutes.

And if you mention a book, that's great.

And really – why not try something impossible, you know?

Because I once saw the playwright Paula Vogel give a talk.

And she said she always tries to put one impossible thing in each play.

And then she said that there was only one truly impossible thing in the theater:

for two people in the audience to have the exact same experience.

And now I know that this is unconventional in a voicemail,

but I'd like to say something personal:

sometimes I lie awake at night wondering what people one hundred years from now will say about us.

About our time on Earth.

They'll look at our art.

Our films.

Our free-to-the-public library events.

And they'll wonder – what were the people of
[   ]¹
thinking?

Were they thinking about the future?

Were they thinking about the present?

Were they numb?

Were they dumb?

Couldn't one little theater troupe have thought of a story to tell?

---

1. The name of the town or city where this play is performed

Scene Two
Opening Night

(**CJ**, **JO**, **RILEY**, *and* **SAM** *are onstage.*)

(*The vibe is: Oh God.*)

RILEY. Did that really just happen?

SAM. What are we supposed to do?

RILEY. We're supposed to be having a party.

CJ. Should we – should there be music?

JO. Is there like – a funeral playlist?

RILEY. Seriously?

CJ. We could have a funeral for my clothes. Everything I'm wearing smells like dog poop.

RILEY. Same.

JO. Yup.

CJ. I mean – that was dog poop tracked all over the stage, right?

JO. No question.

SAM. How did it get there?

RILEY. The devil.

(**TAYLOR** *enters.*)

TAYLOR. OK! Happy Opening!

(**RILEY**, **CJ**, *and* **SAM** *look at* **TAYLOR** *like, "are you kidding me?"*)

What?

JO. Are you serious?

TAYLOR. Yes, come on – time for a toast –

JO. What are we toasting?

TAYLOR. Our play!

JO. Are you – delusional?

TAYLOR. We have to celebrate –

SAM. I made a cake –

CJ. It's lovely –

SAM. Thank you –

JO. OK well I'm sorry, I can't just – stand here and pretend like – that wasn't the most absolutely horrifying ninety minutes of our lives –

TAYLOR. Well, it can't always go as planned, but, all things considered –

JO. All things considered, it was a total catastrophe –

RILEY. I mean, no one died –

JO. No one died! What a consolation.

TAYLOR. Alright well, I think we can all agree that it didn't go as planned, but you know what? We wanted to make a play from scratch, and we made a play from scratch, and I think we deserve to celebrate the fact that we had a lot of good ideas –

JO. But were they good enough to show in public?

CJ. Look, if we're just going to argue, I think – I need to just leave to go see my family – they're waiting in the lobby –

JO. Yeah, and I need to go crawl in a hole –

TAYLOR. Well, wait. Listen. One person saw it. And really liked it.

RILEY. Who?

TAYLOR. The Librarian. Who somehow got my number. And somehow already left an incredibly long voicemail about commissioning a play –

RILEY. A commission!

SAM. What?

CJ. Do you know each other?

JO. Is it paid?

TAYLOR. No. But they're having some event at the library, and the theme is Earth. And the Librarian went on and on in this voicemail about – I don't know – the future? And like – what will future people think? Like what would they think if they looked back at us, and – somehow – our library events?

CJ. Will future people care about our library events?

JO. Do present people care about our library events?

TAYLOR. Anyway, that's the pitch: to tell a story about the Earth.

JO. So let me get this straight: we just experienced total humiliation. Like straight up soul-crushing total humiliation. For the sake of doing theater. And your contribution to this gathering is to do more theater, totally undefined theater, about the entire Earth, for free, for fun.

TAYLOR. Yes.

CJ. And then what?

TAYLOR. And then – I don't know. We disband, we move on. On our own terms. Having done something that we believe in.

JO. Wasn't that the pitch last time?

TAYLOR. Look – we can do this whole – pageant of grievances, we can complain and be jerks and whatever.

But we also need to acknowledge that we promised each other years ago that we were going to make something happen. And we spent so much time waiting for the moment to be right. And then
[

].[2]

And we couldn't make things. And we felt like this was our chance. And we needed to take it.

JO. You needed to take it.

CJ. You opted in, too, Jo.

TAYLOR. And maybe we can think of all of that as some truly terrible rough draft. But we can't just throw away everything – like we made a lot of beautiful stuff happen, too. We did our own rehearsals. We made our own costumes. We figured it all out on our own. And I'm really proud of that, actually.

SAM. Me too.

TAYLOR. And who knows. Maybe this is the last chance we have to make anything together.

And personally I'd rather go out on a high note than fall flat on our faces.

JO. We could very easily fall flat on our faces again.

CJ. Or we could not.

TAYLOR. Exactly. Or we could not.

RILEY. I think this time we need to make something more personal.

---

2. **TAYLOR** says some very real-life reasons why it wasn't possible for them to make a play.

SAM. Like we can be ourselves?

RILEY. I think we were trying too hard to be impressive.

JO. You want to be unimpressive?

RILEY. I want to be real.

SAM. I wouldn't mind having the chance to think about the Earth for the next few weeks.

JO. Do we know anything about the Earth?

RILEY. I know a lot about Uranus.

TAYLOR. Oh my God, Riley –

CJ. Well, whatever. You don't have to do it, Jo.

TAYLOR. Great point, CJ. You don't have to do it, Jo.

SAM. Yeah, if you want to go home, you can.

>   *(A beat.)*

JO. You seriously all want to do this?

>   *(Yes.)*

OK, but it has to be good. Like it has to be a tight ten. Like I'm not going to go out as the company that couldn't even do a really tight ten –

TAYLOR. So we're in?

SAM. I'm in.

CJ. I'm in.

RILEY. I'm in.

TAYLOR. I'm in.

>   *(They look at **JO**.)*

JO. Peer pressure is really messed up, you guys.

Scene Three
The First Rehearsal: Finding A Subject

(CJ is alone in the rehearsal room, preparing to practice something for an invisible audience.)

(At some point during CJ's monologue, SAM enters and listens. CJ doesn't notice.)

CJ. Uhm – OK. So my name is CJ. And I'm going to tell you – OK. So. I got into theater because when I was younger, I loved
[   ].[3]

I really did. I was like – obsessed. I would try to find
[   ][3] everywhere.

And, for whatever reason, my mom thought that we should go see
[   ].[4]

– Oh, I guess a cousin was working on it. So we went to see my cousin's play. And lo and behold, it had all of these
[   ].[3]

And I couldn't believe it. I think my eyes popped out of my head. It was all I could talk about for weeks. Suddenly all I wanted was to grow up and be old enough to do a play. And my mom had to tell me like, CJ, just to be clear, not every play has
[   ].[3]

But I didn't care. I grew up in such a tiny house. In such a massive, massive family. I'm the second youngest of seven. But there's a quality, I think, to watching someone onstage where they can become larger than life. And who wouldn't want the chance to try to be larger than life?

---

3. Something that **CJ** loved
4. The name of a popular show

(CJ suddenly becomes aware of not being alone.)

(CJ sees SAM.)

CJ. Oh my God –

SAM. Hi! Sorry –

CJ. How long have you been there?

SAM. I just walked in –

CJ. Did you hear all of that?

SAM. Are you practicing for something?

CJ. I have this really stupid audition – I mean, it's not stupid, I'm stupid –

SAM. You're not stupid –

CJ. Well whatever, I'm not ready. They want a spontaneous story – and so I'm like – I wrote out twenty spontaneous questions. And I try to do one every day to like –

SAM. Practice being spontaneous?

CJ. Oh no it's even worse when you say it out loud –

SAM. Like what?

CJ. Well today it was – why did you get into theater?

SAM. And what was yesterday?

CJ. Uhm,
[   ]? [5]

SAM. And what'd you say?

CJ. Uh basically
[

                                                                      ]. [6]

---

5. A spontaneous and totally extreme, potentially insane question
6. **CJ**'s response

SAM. Huh –

>   (*Is* **SAM** *impressed? Intrigued? Does* **CJ** *want to disappear?*)

Well – uh – where's the gig?

CJ. I mean, it's not a gig yet. It's over in
[   ].⁷

SAM. Oh. Cool. I know a couple of people out there.

CJ. Wait, you do?

SAM. Yeah, I did a summer festival. I helped on the crew. Nice people –

CJ. God, I can't keep track of all of the like – gigs you've had –

SAM. I've been lucky.

>   (**SAM** *isn't quite sure what to say.*)

>   (*Why is it sometimes so hard to keep talking?*)

CJ. Oh! And – that cake you made for opening was like – really good –

SAM. Oh! Thanks –

CJ. You're like really good at making things –

>   (**TAYLOR**, **JO**, *and* **RILEY** *enter.*)

TAYLOR. Hey – sorry we're late –
[

                                                                    ].⁸

SAM. Again?

TAYLOR. Anyway – circle up?

JO. When is there not a circle.

---

7. Some place that is not quite close, not quite far
8. An excuse about local transportation

(They gather in a circle.)

CJ. Take a breath?

(They take a breath.)

TAYLOR. OK. So. This is the start of a new process. I feel like we have definitely learned some stuff since last time –

JO. Let's hope –

TAYLOR. Can we start with naming some guidelines?

SAM. Sure –

CJ. I think we make something that matters to us.

TAYLOR. Great.

SAM. We have to be able to try stuff.

CJ. Definitely.

RILEY. No ideas are bad ideas.

JO. But we have to make it good.

TAYLOR. And we have to trust the process.

RILEY. Word.

(A beat.)

SAM. And... Where do we start?

TAYLOR. At the beginning, I guess.

CJ. Walk and talk?

JO. About the Earth?

TAYLOR. No ideas are bad ideas.

SAM. Walk and talk!

ALL. Walk and talk!

(And so begins a core company exercise: walk and talk. The goal is to keep moving through the space, filling the space, as they work through a brainstorming process.)

RILEY. So...Earth.

SAM. Earth.

CJ. Earth.

TAYLOR. Earth...

JO. What is the Earth...

SAM. The Earth is
[   ].[9]

CJ. The Earth is
[   ].[10]

TAYLOR. The Earth is
[   ].[11]

RILEY. The Earth is
[   ].[12]

SAM. The Earth is
[   ].[13]

TAYLOR. The Earth is
[   ].[14]

CJ. The Earth is
[   ].[15]

JO. No, but like – *what is the Earth.*

---

9. A broad thing that the Earth is.
10. Another broad thing that the Earth is
11. Another broad thing that the Earth is
12. Another broad thing that the Earth is
13. Another broad thing that the Earth is
14. Another broad thing that the Earth is
15. Another broad thing that the Earth is

SAM. Jump!

ALL. Jump!

> *(They jump. They land. They resume walking.)*

RILEY. OK...the Earth is...
    [   ].[16]

SAM. And the Earth is
    [   ].[17]

CJ. Yeah – the Earth is
    [   ].[18]

TAYLOR. The Earth is
    [   ].[19]

JO. The Earth is
    [   ].[20]

TAYLOR. OK –

SAM. Change direction!

ALL. Change direction!

> *(They change the direction they're walking in.)*

RILEY. Uh – the Earth is...everything. And it came from... nothing?

JO. Literally what does that mean.

CJ. Big Swish!

ALL. Big Swish!

> *(They stop walking and do a company dance move: the Big Swish. It looks like whatever you want it to look like.)*

---

16. A broad, scientific thing that the Earth is
17. Another broad, scientific thing that the Earth is
18. Another broad, scientific thing that the Earth is
19. Another broad, scientific thing that the Earth is
20. Another broad, scientific thing that the Earth is, but with a really depressing twist

JO. Did you hear that
   [

                                                               ]? [21]

CJ. Jo –

TAYLOR. What? Is that true?

JO. Yeah – and it's because
   [

                                                               ]. [22]

RILEY. But what about all of that like –
   [

                                                               ]. [23]

JO. I'm just saying what I heard –

SAM. Expand?

ALL. Expand!

(They briefly expand.)

TAYLOR. OK, let's take it back to the Earth, uhm – where
   did the Earth – come from?

RILEY. [

                                                               ] [24]

---

21. A truly depressing fact about climate crisis
22. JO explains what caused the depressing fact to happen.
23. Something that might counteract Jo's depressing fact
24. A pretty decent explanation of where the Earth came from in
scientific terms. **RILEY** clearly has a handle on the science.

JO. So we're – talking about
[   ]?²⁵

SAM. I don't know, show me
[   ].²⁵

ALL. [   ].²⁵

>   *(They briefly embody the minor detail that Jo
>   mentioned.)*

TAYLOR. Change direction!

ALL. Change direction!

>   *(They change direction.)*

JO. I'm sorry, I don't really feel connected to
[   ].²⁵

SAM. Trust the process –

JO. But I want to feel connected to what we make –

TAYLOR. OK – well. Where are we. On Earth.

RILEY. [

]²⁶

JO. But see that's like huge –

SAM. [

]²⁷

JO. And that's like – so small –

TAYLOR. OK Goldilocks, where are we?

---

25. Some really minor detail from Riley's story
26. A very large, sweeping way of describing where they are
27. A very specific, precise way of describing where they are

JO. OK well, we are
  [   ].[28]

TAYLOR. OK – and where is
  [   ]? [28]

RILEY. 100 miles from
  [   ].[29]

CJ. Huh. I didn't know that.

TAYLOR. Tiny Turkey!

ALL. Tiny Turkey!

> *(Like Big Swish, the Tiny Turkey is a company*
> *dance move. It looks like whatever you want*
> *it to look like. They finish and keep walking.)*

CJ. Well [   ] [28]
  is [   ].[30]

SAM. And [   ] [28]
  is [   ]. [31]

TAYLOR. Show me
  [   ].[31a]

ALL. [   ]! [31a]

> *(They briefly perform the body of water that*
> **SAM** *mentioned.)*

JO. Do we really think that
  [   ] [28]
  is interesting?

TAYLOR. We're exploring –

---

28. What feels like a medium-sized way of describing where they are: a
town, a neighborhood, a county, etc.
29. A landmark that they're one hundred miles from
30. Describe a relationship to a large geographical feature that is not
water.
31. Describe a relationship to a body, or bodies, of water.
31a. Body of water that **SAM** mentioned

JO. We should do something about like
[   ].³²

SAM. Jo, could you show us
[   ]?³²

(**JO** *tries to show what* **JO** *just talked about.*)

JO. I mean – it's just a draft –

RILEY. No apologies.

CJ. Jump!

ALL. Jump!

(*They jump and keep moving.*)

RILEY. I want to go back to where we are.

SAM. OK –

RILEY. Can we name twenty species that live here?

JO. Twenty?

RILEY. Yes.

SAM. Uh –
[

]³³

TAYLOR. [

]³⁴

CJ. [

]³⁵

JO. I literally cannot think of one.

---

32. Something really big, intense and dramatic that's happening because
of climate crisis
33. Species 1, 2, 3
34. Species 4, 5, 6
35. Species 7, 8, 9

RILEY. [

]³⁶

JO. Riley – what?

SAM. Show me [   ].^{36a}

> (**RILEY** *shows Species 15.*)

RILEY. [

]³⁷

JO. OK wow –

SAM. How many is that?

TAYLOR. Fifteen –

CJ. OK – [   ]³⁸

RILEY. [

]³⁹

SAM. That's nineteen –

TAYLOR. [   ]⁴⁰

> (*And I should note: Species 20 is an easy one.*)

RILEY. Show me [   ].⁴⁰

ALL. [   ]!⁴⁰

> (*They briefly perform Species 20.*)

---

36. Species 10, 11, 12, 13, 14, 15. And these feel like – advanced species.
36a. From **36:** Species 15
37. A very brief explanation of what the species is
38. Species 16
39. Species 17, 18, 19
40. Species 20

CJ. Change direction?

ALL. Change direction!

    (They change direction.)

JO. OK well, humans are also here –

RILEY. And how did we get here?

    (And ideally, the following responses incorporate many different scales of how they got there. Some may span billions of years. Some may span ten minutes. Some may incorporate very personal family history. Some may incorporate broader generational context. But these answers should brief, like a sentence or two.)

CJ. [

                                         ] [41]

  Sam?

SAM. [

                                         ] [42]

  Taylor?

TAYLOR. [

                                         ] [43]

  Riley?

---

41. **CJ** says how **CJ** got there.
42. **SAM** says how **SAM** got there.
43. **TAYLOR** says how **TAYLOR** got there.

RILEY. [

]⁴⁴

　Jo?

JO. [

]⁴⁵

TAYLOR. Change direction?

ALL. Change direction.

　　(They change direction.)

JO. So...

RILEY. You know what? Here's a story about the Earth. The Earth is a planet that has fish.

　And the craziest fish, to me, is the deep sea angler fish.

　　(And if, for whatever reason, the tale of the deep sea angler fish presents content obstacles, you may select another story of another species, just make sure that it is a freaky and unexpected story.)

SAM. Story!

ALL. Story!

　　*(Perhaps they all freeze to listen to **RILEY.**)*

RILEY. This is the story of the deep sea angler fish. It's the one with the lantern. Or – the female has a lantern.

---

44. RILEY says how **RILEY** got there.
45. JO says how **JO** got there. And **JO**'s story involves something intense because **JO** keeps things intense.

The female has everything. And the female is huge. And the male is small. The male is small and pathetic. And the female roams the seas with her lantern, [   ]⁴⁶ and the male is like ah! I can't do anything! But the female needs the male in order to make her babies. And that female is smart. She knows that basically the only sense he has is smell. So she makes herself smell like food. Like – emits the smell of food. And so the male swims up to her and tries to take a bite! But before he can eat her, she traps him! And she makes him fuse with her body for all of time. And she can get like – as many of these as she wants. And they just become like her own little personal sperm machines. And she makes her babies. And she lives her life. And that's the story of the deep sea angler fish.

CJ. WOW.

JO. Jump?

ALL. Jump!

(They jump.)

TAYLOR. OK I like this, I think this is good. I think we should all tell a story about a part of nature that we are completely obsessed with.

CJ. I don't have any stories like Riley –

TAYLOR. That's OK. It can be simple. Like I'm obsessed with [   ].⁴⁷

CJ. OK – I'm obsessed with [

---

46. A word or phrase that means "having the time of your life"
47. TAYLOR says something that **TAYLOR**'s obsessed with.

].⁴⁸

JO. Well I'm obsessed with
  [

].⁴⁹

  Do you like – want to do a play about that?

CJ. I don't.

JO. OK.

RILEY. How about deep sea angler fish?

JO. No.

TAYLOR. When I was a kid I was obsessed with
  [   ].⁵⁰

CJ. My mom's obsessed with
  [   ].⁵¹

JO. I'm obsessed with your mom.

SAM. OK I don't know if this is too simple, but I'm obsessed with...
  [   ].⁵²

  *(And this is very important: what **SAM** says is something local, simple, and close to all of them.)*

JO. That's it?

---

48. **CJ** tells a very brief story about something that **CJ** is obsessed with.
49. And **JO** says something kind of depressing.
50. A thing **TAYLOR** was obsessed with
51. Something CJ's mom is obsessed with
52. **SAM** says something simple.

SAM. Yeah.

JO. OK –

CJ. I mean I love
[   ]⁵²
too.

(*And it's possible that what* **SAM** *says will be straightforward, like seagulls. But it's possible that the subject will be a little less straightforward, like a particular path in the woods. In the event that a little more clarity is helpful to identify the subject, feel free to add these lines:*)

CJ. *You mean [*   *].*⁵²ᵃ

SAM. *Yes –*

(*Whether you add those lines or not, pick back up here.*)

CJ. [

]⁵³

RILEY. I mean – [

]⁵⁴

TAYLOR. Wait – is this – it?

52a. CJ says one way to clarify or specify what **SAM** has said
53. CJ tells a brief story about an experience **CJ** has had of what Sam said.
54. RILEY tells a brief story about why **RILEY** loves what Sam said.

JO. What does that mean?

TAYLOR. Is this what our play is about?

JO. No –

TAYLOR. But go with me – like the Earth is too big, the Earth is too overwhelming, and wasn't that the problem last time? That what we talked about was just too big?

JO. So from the whole Earth, we're going to talk about
[   ].⁵²

TAYLOR. Why not?

CJ. I mean we only have ten minutes.

SAM. I would love to do ten minutes on
[   ].⁵²

RILEY. Yeah, I mean, if you think about it,
[   ]⁵²
is a part of [   ]⁵⁵
and [   ]⁵⁵
is part of the Earth, and so therefore, by talking about
[   ],⁵²
we are talking about the Earth.

JO. Right but like – why would we talk about
[   ]⁵²
when we could be talking about
[

                                                    ]⁵⁶

TAYLOR. Jo –

JO. I mean honestly – why not?

---

55. Where they live
56. JO names a storm that happened in their area last year. It's important that this is the same kind of storm that happens later in the play. **JO** should name a consequence or two of that storm.

CJ. That's really heavy –

JO. And?

TAYLOR. And our last show was like – very heavy –

JO. But don't we want to talk about something that *means* something?

TAYLOR. Well isn't that what's actually – sort of radical? To say that [   ] 52 means something? To all of us? To make the ordinary extraordinary –

CJ. Don't you have a story about
[   ]? 52

JO. Yes, obviously, who doesn't?

[

] 57

– but if the point of this is like – posterity? For the future? You want future people to think that we were just so obsessed with
[   ]? 58

TAYLOR. Riley, could you expand on your story? About
[   ]? 52

RILEY. Uh, sure –

[

---

57. **JO** shares the briefest, unimpressive anecdote related to what Sam said.
58. A sort of diminutive, judgy way to describe what Sam said

]⁵⁹

TAYLOR. I'm telling you – there's something there –

CJ. I'm game.

RILEY. Yup.

TAYLOR. Jo –

JO. Come on –

TAYLOR. I'm serious. Trust me.

RILEY. Trust the process.

TAYLOR. OK?

JO. OK –

ALL. OK –

[   ]⁵²

---

59. RILEY tells a short story – around five sentences – about what Sam said. Perhaps this is a story about the first time that **RILEY** noticed, or felt connected to it. It feels personal and simple, and somehow very beautiful because of its simplicity.

Scene Four
The Second Rehearsal: Object Work

(The Rehearsal Room. The next day.)

(They have each brought in two objects that remind them of the subject. Some of these objects can be very literal. But some of them should be a stretch. **SAM** *has brought a light source of some kind.)*

TAYLOR. OK, so does everyone have their objects?

RILEY. Yup.

TAYLOR. Shall we start with a quick show and tell? Sam, wanna start?

SAM. Sure. [

]60

CJ?

CJ. [

---

60. **SAM** talks about two objects, and why **SAM** chose to bring them in.

]⁶¹

Taylor?

TAYLOR. [

]⁶² Riley?

RILEY. [

]⁶³ Jo?

---

61. CJ talks about two objects, and why **CJ** chose to bring them in.
62. TAYLOR talks about two objects, and why **TAYLOR** chose to bring them in.
63. RILEY talks about two objects, and why **RILEY** chose to bring them in.

JO. [

][64]

TAYLOR. Huh.

JO. What.

TAYLOR. Nothing, I just wouldn't have thought of
     [   ].[64a]

JO. I thought no ideas were bad ideas.

SAM. Well anyway – should we start working? Are we
     ready to play scene?

RILEY. Can we go over the rules again?

TAYLOR. Basically – the objects are here. This is the stage.
     We're over here. And we come up and make stuff – and
     see what happens.

CJ. Can we do lights and sound?

TAYLOR. If you want. Let's feel it out.

          (**SAM** *adjusts the lights, perhaps starts to
          play a little music.*[*])

     OK. Everybody ready? Scene –

ALL. Scene!

---

64. JO talks about two objects, and why JO chose to bring them in.
64a. Something from 64: what JO has brought
[*] A license to produce *To Tell A Story About the Earth* does not include
a performance license for any third-party or copyrighted recordings.
Licensees should create their own.

(They set up to play Scene by placing each of their objects on a table. They begin to play Scene. And here is how to play Scene, which is adapted from Tectonic Theater Project's Moment Work. Everyone sits in the "audience" facing the "stage," which is where the objects are. One by one, they each get up to create a small moment with one or more of the objects. This could mean doing something amazing and unexpected with time, or light, or a crossing, or duration, or animating an object in a mesmerizing way. It should feel like they are allowing the objects to do the work of performance and storytelling. There can be some murmurs of oooh and ah when they see something that really works, but otherwise, this exercise should be done without language or dialogue.)

(After what feels like one round...)

TAYLOR. Okay, and could you start to show me
[   ]⁵²?
And could we start to do multiple people?

(A few people at a time animate the objects again, but this time trying to evoke their subject. But – it's not quite there. And it probably feels really weird.)

*(At some point, **JO** asks:)*

JO. What does this have to do with the Earth?

TAYLOR. Jo, be quiet.

RILEY. Trust.

*(The last person to go up is **SAM**. And **SAM** has a good idea.)*

SAM. CJ, could you come up here? And could you tell the story that you told yesterday about

[   ],[52]

but like – expand it a little? Like – spontaneously?

    (*A private wink. Yes.*)

CJ. [

][65]

    (*As* **CJ** *tells the story,* **SAM** *makes a final gesture: something gorgeous and simple with light. For example: using one of the objects to cast a surprising, evocative shadow.*)

    (*And when* **SAM** *puts the light source and the object together, it starts to really evoke the subject – either because of the texture the light casts, or the shadow, or some unexpected image. The juxtaposition of* **SAM**'s *image and* **CJ**'s *story feels incredibly exciting.*)

---

65. A short story – about seven sentences – elaborating on **53:** the story **CJ** told at the end of the previous scene. It is simple and personal, which feels profound.

(When **CJ**'s *story is over,* **CJ** *says:)*

CJ. Scene.

SAM. Scene.

TAYLOR. I feel like we just saw the play.

SAM. Keep going?

(Yes.)

(And then, time passes.)

Scene Five
The Seventh Rehearsal: Things Fall Apart

(We hear a little bit of sound: the beginnings of a storm. This storm will take whatever form is relevant for the place where you set the play: a hurricane, an ice storm, a blizzard, etc. We could hear wind, rain, branches of trees... whatever makes the most sense for where you are.)

*(**TAYLOR** is in the room alone, preparing for rehearsal. Perhaps **TAYLOR** is putting up giant Post-Its or butcher paper or a whiteboard or notecards to help them track their scenes. These can be the materials that you have used in the process of making your own ten-minute play. **RILEY** enters.)*

RILEY. Oh wow, what's this?

TAYLOR. Uh – I thought this might help us put together the show? Like – I think we're at the point where we can start putting different little moments in order –

RILEY. Are you sure we're going to be able to rehearse?

TAYLOR. Why wouldn't we be able to rehearse?

RILEY. This [   ] [66]
seems to be really picking up –

TAYLOR. I don't think it'll be that bad.

RILEY. Really?

TAYLOR. Yeah. I mean, you never really know with weather these days –

---

66. Kind of storm

RILEY. Well the last time we had one of these, my family lost power for like four days, and that's really not good. And I was looking at the news and I was reading about how [

].[67]

TAYLOR. Woah.

RILEY. Yeah.

TAYLOR. You know, I think I somehow didn't realize how into science you are...

RILEY. Oh yeah. I mean – it's what I want to do.

TAYLOR. Seriously? Like – with your life?

RILEY. Yeah –

TAYLOR. Then why are you hanging out with us?

RILEY. Because, I don't know – theater is fun.

TAYLOR. Wow.

RILEY. But I think you could like – do this if you wanted to. I think you really are a good leader, Taylor.

TAYLOR. Aren't we all the leader?

(RILEY *shrugs.*)

---

67. RILEY talks in a slightly elevated scientific way about local conditions that would make a storm particularly brutal. How dry the ground is, or how full the rivers are, how temperature is impacting weather patterns, or possible consequences: mudslides, big tides, overflowing drainage, how extreme temperatures could impact the energy grid, etc. Make it relevant to your area.

RILEY. I just like the way you see things.

(**CJ**, **SAM**, *and* **JO** *enter.*)

JO. Wow, it is really not looking good out there –

TAYLOR. We'll be fine.

RILEY. What's happening now?

SAM. [

]⁶⁸

RILEY. Oh shoot –

TAYLOR. Well I think we're on the verge of a breakthrough. So I think if we could just – push through –

JO. *(Re: the materials that* **TAYLOR** *has prepared.)* What are all of these?

TAYLOR. Well, we're midway through our process, and we have a lot of amazing stuff, like a lot of incredible moments, and – I feel like we have to take a step back and lock down an actual shape –

SAM. Didn't we say we wanted to start with
[   ]?⁶⁹

TAYLOR. Great –

CJ. And I feel like the ending is obviously
[   ].⁷⁰

RILEY. Yes –

JO. But what does that mean?

TAYLOR. What do you mean what does it mean?

---

68. **SAM** describes what it looks or feels like outside.
69. **SAM** names a moment that they have come up with as a group. This could be like "the Growth of the Big Tree." It should be a moment that does end up in your final play, so fill this part in after you've figured it all out.
70. **CJ** names another moment that they have come up with.

JO. People will just watch
   [   ][69]
   then like – [   ],[71]
   then [   ],[70]
   and that's it?

SAM. I think that'd be awesome –

JO. But what does that say? Like – there has to be a point, right?

CJ. Can't the point be beauty?

RILEY. I thought the point was how much we love
   [   ].[52]

JO. Yeah, and honestly, what does that have to do with anything that's happening?

TAYLOR. Haven't we been over this?

JO. No seriously, what does it have to do with emergency?

SAM. Maybe we should actually take a step back and think about what we want the audience to feel?

RILEY. I want them to feel amazed. Because I think that people deserve some amazement.

JO. Fine. And I want them to feel like we understand that we're living in crisis.

RILEY. Like we're doomed?

JO. I mean, tell me we're not.

TAYLOR. But what does that *do*, telling people we're doomed?

JO. I don't know, but that's the truth –

CJ. I think we should give people a reason to be hopeful –

JO. About what?

CJ. About the future. About our lives –

---

71. The name of yet another moment.

JO. But that's ridiculous –

CJ. Why is it any more ridiculous than wanting people to feel doomed?

JO. Because it isn't real! What if there is actually no hope? What if what's happening right now – in the world – it's not just something that someone can just – swoop in and fix –

TAYLOR. There is absolutely stuff to fix.

JO. But there isn't like – a silver bullet. Recycle and everything will just work out. That's not real –

CJ. Who said that recycling will save us?

TAYLOR. Who said this was about recycling?

SAM. We're trying to say something about
[   ].⁵²

JO. And is that because we all just like – randomly have a story? I mean
[   ]⁵²
is fine, like on its own but –

TAYLOR. Do you mean: should we even be making this play?

JO. Well – maybe. Yeah.

CJ. We were asked to put on a play –

JO. And maybe we should have asked ourselves right at the beginning – what is the point?

CJ. To do something nice for the Library!

JO. See, that is not like a reason. To do something nice. When the world is falling apart.

RILEY. Jo –

CJ. So you like – need to stop the world from falling apart?

TAYLOR. With a ten-minute play?

RILEY. Ambitious.

JO. How am I the only person who thinks that we have to like – say something real?

CJ. We're telling real stories about
[   ].⁵²

JO. But what is the point! Like what does it all add up to!

SAM. Do you need to take a break?

TAYLOR. That's a great idea.

JO. No. We can't just shut things down the minute they get interesting.

TAYLOR. You mean heated.

JO. I mean real.

TAYLOR. OK, but look – we don't have time to make this about everything –

JO. That is what I mean! Exactly! We do not have time! There is no time! Like there has been no time for a long time, and there's definitely no time now. Like there was time, like in the 80s, like there was time, like in the 90s and the 2000s, and every year, we just lose time, and we're losing time, and we're losing time, like I have this reoccurring nightmare that we're standing in front of these – gates of time – and we're watching them close, and I'm calling out like hey hey hey hey the gates are closing, I'm watching them close, hurry up or we won't get through – and like let's be clear – it's not like if we get out, we're good – it's like, we'll still have an unbelicvable amount of suffering – like we'll still have like this amount of uninhabitable places and like this amount of species loss and this amount of like – a hundred foot tidal waves because the best case scenario is still a global emergency, and like not to mention everything else that happens when people are hot and tired and desperate, like not even accounting for war, like not even – like if we can't do – enough – then literally what is anything?

(And suddenly their emergency alerts start to go off on their phones.)

CJ. What is that – what's happening –

(They run to their phones.)

TAYLOR. It's saying [

].[72]

RILEY. I need to get home.

CJ. We all do –

SAM. Is that safe?

RILEY. It's only going to get worse –

(They scramble to get out of there as quickly as they can.)

TAYLOR. Jo – wait –

JO. I've gotta go –

(And everyone leaves.)

---

72. Something the alert would say about the extreme weather event beginning, and a directive to take certain precautions. Their conclusion should be that they have to go home.

Scene Six
The Storm

(In the dark, we hear the storm.)

(It is, indeed, a very scary storm.)

Scene Seven
What Do We Do?

(SAM sits in the empty room. SAM makes something beautiful happen with a design element. CJ comes in and watches. SAM doesn't notice immediately.)

CJ. That's beautiful –

SAM. CJ!

CJ. Sorry if I startled you –

SAM. No, it's –

CJ. Are you OK? Did you get home OK last night?

SAM. [

]73

CJ. Oh no –

SAM. How about you?

CJ. [

]74

SAM. No –

CJ. Well it's better than what happened in
     [   ].75

SAM. I couldn't believe the pictures I saw –

CJ. Yeah. And the trees in
     [   ].76
     That's like – hundreds of years of trees –

---

73. **SAM** describes something difficult that happened on the way home.
74. **CJ** says something that happened to **CJ**'s home, and it's actually quite serious.
75. A place nearby that was really damaged
76. A place nearby that might have really old trees

SAM. [   ]⁷⁷
    fell right next to us. Smashed like – three cars –

CJ. Did it smash your car?

SAM. Luckily, no.

    (A beat.)

    (They try to figure out how to deal with this moment.)

But uhm – how was your audition? With the spontaneous story?

CJ. Oh – I didn't get it.

SAM. Oh, CJ – No!

CJ. Whatever. It's fine. It's probably for the best – I should probably just get a real job –

SAM. But that is a real job –

CJ. No, but I mean – something stable. That I can rely on – something that can help me support myself, support my family.

SAM. But it's your dream –

CJ. I mean – yeah. I love this. Of course I love this, but I just feel like suddenly – everything that was solid isn't solid? Like – everything I thought I could rely on is uhm – and I mean, even though we all like – agreed – that it like really sucked to be alone, that it was better to make stuff together, but there's actually, like, not really a together? And we can't get along? And everyone just leaves?

    (A beat.)

    *(**SAM** doesn't quite know what to say.)*

I'm sorry. Last night was intense. But – uh – how about you? Do you know what you're doing after this?

---

77. Something that could fall

SAM. Well actually, I got into the Drama Program at
[   ].[78]

CJ. Wait – what? Really?

SAM. Yeah. I heard last week.

CJ. Sam! Wow – that's amazing –

SAM. Thanks –

CJ. Wow. Jeeze! That's huge! That's – you're big-leagues!

SAM. We'll see –

CJ. No, you are. I know you are. You really are. You're
gonna like – make it –

> *(And they look at each other.)*

> *(And **CJ** is trying so hard to be happy.)*

> *(But we see **CJ**'s heart break.)*

When do you leave?

SAM. I still have a couple of months. And CJ – I don't just
want to leave you behind.

CJ. What does that mean?

SAM. It means – I don't know. That I think you're incredible?

CJ. What?

SAM. Yeah. It means I think you're like – kind and
thoughtful and talented –

CJ. Sam –

SAM. And I want to like – cook for you sometime? Like –
I could make you dinner?

CJ. Like – a date?

SAM. Uhm – would you like that?

---

78. A place that feels far away and impressive

CJ. Would I like it to be dinner, or would I like it to be a date?

SAM. Like – both?

>   *(Ah!)*

CJ. Uhm. Yeah. I'd like that. I'd really like that –

SAM. OK cool –

CJ. Yeah. Cool –

>   *(Are they about to kiss?????????)*

>   *(But just then, everyone else comes in.)*

RILEY. Are you kissing?????

CJ. What! No!

TAYLOR. Everybody OK in here?

SAM. Yes, we're fine –

JO. Did you guys see

>   [   ]?[76]

CJ. Yeah, we were just talking about that –

JO. I heard

>   [

>   ].[79]

RILEY. That's crazy –

TAYLOR. Yeah, our friend

>   [

>   ].[80]

---

79. JO elaborates on what went wrong in **76**, and the impact it's having.
80. A short anecdote about something really crazy that happened in the storm

CJ. No way –

JO. That's awful.

RILEY. My family lost power –

SAM. Oh no –

RILEY. Not good –

TAYLOR. Well – I don't really know where we should start today –

JO. Why not.

>   (**TAYLOR** *looks at* **JO.**)

TAYLOR. Should we – take a breath?

>   (*They take a breath.*)

I mean we obviously had a tough rehearsal yesterday – and a lot has happened and I just feel like – I don't really know where to start –

>   (*And there's a beat.*)

>   (*No one really knows where to start.*)

>   (**TAYLOR** *summons the courage to tell the truth.*)

I mean, as I was trying to get home last night, I actually was thinking about what you were saying, Jo. About the gates. And you're right. I feel that, too. And I think we have to make a piece where something is really at stake –

JO. Really?

TAYLOR. Yeah –

JO. Well, I was thinking last night about how maybe [   ] 52
is at stake in like – a real way.

[

]⁸¹

CJ. Well when you put it like that –

TAYLOR. Walk?

ALL. Walk.

(They walk.)

RILEY. OK, well I also have something to say. And I would like us to keep walking.

(They keep walking. But as **RILEY** *tells the story below, perhaps their walking becomes slower, more contemplative. They are really listening to* **RILEY**'s *story.)*

Maybe you know this, maybe you don't. My dad is sick.

JO. I didn't know that.

RILEY. Well. He is. He's had a brain tumor since I was born. And when I was born they did a surgery, and they thought they got it, but it's back. And it's worse now. And it's been taking up so much of the good parts about my family's life. But you know what I learned? You can't just mope around wishing things were different. And wishing that people – or anything – could be permanent. Because nothing is permanent. But guess what? We're alive. And that is so important. And I think that we have to keep reminding people of that. That it is beautiful just to be alive. Even when bad things happen. Even when we think we are doomed.

---

81. JO explains how, in a real way, the subject they have chosen is a part of the larger story of our climate emergency, and perhaps has a lesson to offer about resilience, or ingenuity, or the fragile beauty of our ecosystem, or what we risk losing.

JO. Riley, I had no idea –

RILEY. Well, don't pity me, just get over yourself. And like – make something my dad would enjoy. And for the record, he loves
[   ].⁵²

(And then **THE LIBRARIAN** *enters.)*

THE LIBRARIAN. Hello – is this – rehearsal?

SAM. Who are you?

THE LIBRARIAN. I'm the Librarian.

CJ. Oh!

RILEY. Wow!

JO. Is everything OK?

THE LIBRARIAN. Haven't you heard?
[

                                                        ] ⁸²

JO. What?

THE LIBRARIAN. So we have to cancel the show. And everything else.

SAM. Like – there's no more Library?

TAYLOR. There has to be something we can do –

THE LIBRARIAN. Ha! Do you have five million dollars?

---

82. THE LIBRARIAN explains three terrible things that happened to the library because of the storm: at least one structural thing that happened, and two important things that were lost as a result.

*(A beat in which everyone wishes very much
that they had five million dollars.)*

I'm sorry – I've just –

I've poured my heart and soul into helping people read,
and helping people learn, and just trying to be a force
for some sort of public good – and it just –

I mean, nothing is permanent. Nothing is given. And
maybe nothing can be a library forever –

JO. We have to do something.

CJ. Like a fundraiser?

RILEY. Yeah, what if we did a fundraiser?

THE LIBRARIAN. Where?

TAYLOR. Here? An evening for the library? And we could
do our play?

THE LIBRARIAN. You would still – do your play?

JO. Theater is notoriously lucrative.

THE LIBRARIAN. You really would?

JO. I mean – yeah. Wouldn't we?

TAYLOR. Yes.

CJ. Absolutely –

*(And if there are more people you'd like to
have in your final play, you can add these
lines:)*

SAM. *And I have some friends who can help us, too.*

TAYLOR. *Great!*

SAM. Do you want to join us? For rehearsal?

THE LIBRARIAN. Really?

RILEY. Stay. Ten minutes.

TAYLOR. We'll show you what we've got.

Scene Eight
The Next Few Weeks

(Time passes.)

(They prepare.)

(And let's have a little bit of music.*)

---

* A license to produce *To Tell A Story About the Earth* does not include a performance license for any third-party or copyrighted recordings. Licensees should create their own.

Scene Nine
The Performance

(**THE LIBRARIAN** *enters.*)

THE LIBRARIAN. Hi, everyone!

Welcome to our Library Fundraiser.

I'm so proud that today we can present the work of these inspired, artistic people.

I honestly – I never expected this.

And I am just – so incredibly moved – that these young people would want to – dedicate their efforts for the sake of our dear Library.

Which is currently, of course, not so much of a Library.

So please – if you, like these artists, believe that there is value in what the Library does, or what the Library stands for, or if you have ever wanted to simply learn something, and found a way to learn it, then please. Donate what you can.

Because it's been very hard, as of late, to be a Librarian. But I do believe that what we do has very deep value.

Because a Library is a community.

Sort of like a theater.

And for the record, some people in this town are very skeptical about my love for the theater.

So I thought I ought to address that.

I believe in the theater because it's something you must do with others.

And it's something you must practice.

And it's something that, a lot of times, you have to invent from thin air.

I don't know how to articulate the meaning of our lives.

But I can tell you this – I'm grateful to these young people.

So in conclusion: read a book.

And let's all just – do what we can to be good to each other.

Thank you.

Now please enjoy

[   ].[83]

 (**THE LIBRARIAN** *joins the audience.*)

 (*And then the performance begins.*)

 (**TAYLOR**, **CJ**, **SAM**, **JO**, *and* **RILEY** *– and perhaps a* **CHORUS OF THEIR FRIENDS** *– enter and present their play. They tell the story of their subject. They use objects that they have brought in. They use gesture, and movement, and light. We see glimpses of moments we've seen them rehearse, and when we see it all together it feels like a revelation. They find a way to weave together their personal stories to tell the story of their subject, and what it means to them. It can be very playful. They can try something impossible! There are no rules! But the fact that it is very specific, and very personal, makes it somehow feel universal and expansive. At the end of the play, we feel that it is extraordinary and beautiful to be alive all together. We believe that there is so much worth fighting for, and that love gives all effort meaning.*)

 (*Please insert your beautiful script here:*)

---

83. The title of the play that you have made

(The performance ends.)

(**THE LIBRARIAN** *goes wild.*)

(**THE LIBRARIAN** *leaps back up on the stage.*)

THE LIBRARIAN. I have no words –

RILEY. None needed.

THE LIBRARIAN. The part with the –
    [   ].[84]

SAM. That started as
    [   ].[85]

THE LIBRARIAN. And then the bit with the –
    [   ].[86]

CJ. That was Jo.

THE LIBRARIAN. And I truly didn't expect that something so simple could say so much.

JO. Well – we live to surprise.

THE LIBRARIAN. How should we celebrate?

JO. I uhm – I brought some cake?

TAYLOR. You did?

JO. Yeah.

TAYLOR. Like – a gesture?

JO. I guess so.

SAM. You always need cake.

JO. Exactly. And I, uh, just want to say – thanks for doing all of this. For like – keeping us together.

TAYLOR. You know we love you, right?

---

84. A part in the play
85. A very small seed of an idea
86. A prop they used

JO. Sucks to be you.

> *(And* **JO** *looks at* **TAYLOR**, *at everyone.* **JO** *loves these people.)*

Happy opening.

ALL. Happy opening.

The End

A NOTE ON PROCESS FROM LUBDUB THEATRE CO.

As a company, we recognize and celebrate that every ensemble has its own way of working. Each production of this play will be unique: every cast will fill in the blanks with their own original words, and each ten-minute performance will honor a different local spot or species.

With that acknowledged, we also want to share some tips that have worked for us through the script's development. It has been especially helpful to think about the creative process sequentially, in the five phases detailed below. Please feel free to follow these instructions in whatever way works best for you. The most important thing, as Miranda notes in her Author's Notes, is to choose a nearby part of the world that you care deeply about, and to let that Subject – and that care – be your creative guides.

1. Get to know the characters and their world before filling in the blanks.

The chance to add your own voice to the script represents a unique opportunity to showcase your particular sense of humor, interests, and concerns within the context of the play. Actors often cannot wait to rise to this challenge, showcasing their improvisational skills by filling in the blanks right away. We have found, however, that it can be helpful not to jump immediately into these decisions. Instead, we recommend you take a bit of time to learn, together, how each blank functions in the context of the characters' individual voices and the overall mechanics of the story.

Especially during a first read-through, we recommend that actors actually read each prompt aloud as if it were part of the line, rather than filling in the blanks on the fly. For example, in Scene 3, **CJ** would say "when I was younger, I loved 'something that **CJ** loved.'" This placeholder might sound a little silly at first, but it opens up important space for learning about the characters. Who are these young artists? What distinguishes each of their individual voices? What are their personal interests, and what attracts them to the group's collective way of working? The words that you ultimately choose to fill in the blanks will represent a fusion of the actor's voice and the character's particular circumstances and style. (For example, each Riley will be unique, but every **RILEY** has a special interest in science.)

This approach also teaches you about the play as a whole. Listen for the ways that the blanks function in the scene. Is this space for a punchline, or do we need to work together to keep up the pace? Should this answer be surprising, or should it feel tied to surrounding lines? Think about how your answers will flow within the play's broader patterns.

2. Answer the "Pre-Devising" (1–51) and "Storm" Prompts (65–68, 72–80, 86).

Once you have met the characters and gotten a sense of how their story unfolds, begin to experiment with possible answers for the blanks. Start with this first set: these are the prompts that establish the world of the play and don't specifically reference your ten-minute performance or its Subject (that's Step 3). This is also a good time to decide on the type of storm that will strike in Scenes 5–6.

This first working pass is a good time to improvise. Change it up: experiment with some answers that feel logical and others that surprise you and make you laugh. Lean into spontaneity and play, while remembering everything you've learned about the characters. In our process, after we improvised for a couple days, we made time for everyone to sit with a pencil and their scripts, penciling in first-draft answers for the blanks in their own lines. We then shared these experiments in a second table read. We left time to discuss and revise, emphasizing opportunities to amplify humor, clarity, and specificity.

This process should feel like a collective creative leap, rather than a test: try out a bunch of options! Refine! Iterate! Erase and rewrite! Don't be afraid to get it "wrong." During rehearsals, you will get a natural sense for which answers are working well and which ones might want to evolve. We recommend making sure that the beginnings and endings of each answer are especially clear, so that everybody can track their cues. Keep an eye, too, on which answers are repeated. For example, the "minor detail in Riley's story" (prompt 25) should be consistent when it is repeated by different characters. Let someone on your team (perhaps a dramaturg, stage manager, or assistant director) help keep everyone on the same page by maintaining a running list of your collective answers to all of the prompts.

3. Choose a Subject and Answer the "Subject Selection" Prompts (52–59, 65–68).

After you've filled in the "Pre-Devising" and "Storm" blanks, choose your Subject! (This is the "Something simple" that Sam names toward the end of Scene 3, which eventually becomes the focus of your ten-minute performance.) Pay special attention here to Miranda's instructions: the subject should be something simple, local, and close to everyone. This proximity should be both geographic and emotional. Pick something that matters to you, and aim for something that everyone on your team has experienced firsthand in some way.

We recommend a democratic process. Once we had a general feel for the play, and some initial ideas about our answers to the Pre-Devising and Storm prompts (Step 2), we organized a "Subject Selection Day." We invited everyone – cast, crew, and creative team – to come to rehearsal with ideas about what the subject might be. The ensemble should bring suggestions that they're excited about but shouldn't try to decide in advance: leave room for collaboration and surprise!

Then, on the "Subject Selection Day," take time for everyone to pitch their ideas. Listen for ripples of recognition. You can tell there's a lot of potential for a subject when everyone can't wait to chime in: "When I was little, I went there all the time!" "I saw one of those this morning!" "Oh my gosh, last summer, I...," etc. These waves of excitement signal that a suggestion has common appeal and will produce lots of material for devising. When all the potential subjects have been pitched, we recommend a vote.

Don't overthink it, or feel you have to stretch. Part of the magic of this work is recognizing the profundity in places, plants, or creatures that we encounter everymday but often fail to consider. For example, in a sharing at Georgetown University, the students chose a brick path that runs beneath a beautiful and ancient ash tree – which, we later found, is threatened by an invasive species of bark-munching beetle. In a workshop in New York City, we selected "bodega cats" as our subject. The more we thought about these neighborhood felines, the more we came to see them as unsung icons of resilience and ingenuity. An ensemble in Franklin, Massachusetts chose the ladybug – a special emblem of their town.

4. Devise Your Ten-Minute Performance.

Once you have landed on a Subject, take time to devise your ten-minute performance. Let your curiosity and passion guide you toward the most resonant material. As an overall goal, we recommend trying to share a story that reflects your ensemble's – or your community's – collective experience of this place or species.

As a starting point, experiment with the exercises portrayed in the play. You can draw on the characters' brainstorming activities in Scene 2: organize a "walk and talk" and see what comes up. Experiment with gestures that evoke your Subject. See what little stories emerge when you place multiple gestures in succession. Often in devising work, a sequence of physical discoveries can move the script forward in exciting ways. (Pay attention to these "Aha!" moments, as you'll have an opportunity to recreate them in Step 5 below.)

Spend a rehearsal doing your own version of the "Object Work" in Scene 4. Ask everyone to bring in two objects that remind them of the Subject in some way, and start by sharing these connections – like a "show and tell." We suggest that you begin this sharing with a declaration of consent. Devising is a collective process, so it's important to acknowledge that any objects, words, or narratives that you share might be handled or rearranged by other members of the team. Think about agreements that make this work feel safe and respectful for all.

After an initial share, devote some time to exploring these objects as they exist in space, and in relation to one another. How do they move? How do they metamorphose with shifts in lights and sound? Start without language, then experiment by layering in some simple words: these could be phrases from the "walk and talk," memories shared in the "show and tell," descriptions of the Subject itself, or new ideas. But don't forget the basics: where is the Subject found? What does it do, or what happens there, at different times of day? The verbal, visual, and emotional textures of all these answers will inform the work that you will build together.

As you explore, look for glimmers of personal connection: When did you experience the Subject for the first time? When did you experience it most recently? What challenges does the Subject face, and how might it overcome them? If you're interested in speaking about a particular challenge, look for ways to frame it in personal terms. If your Subject has undergone some kind of shift in recent seasons (or centuries), how have you and your family experienced this change?

With a personal foundation in place, we also encourage you to explore other voices that might have something to say about the Subject. These could be historical, or scientific: do elders in your community have memories they might like to share? Do any interesting accounts of the Subject exist in your local library, archives, or lab? In our company, we are often interested in the idea of a "Chorus" that helps move the action forward. These voices don't always have to be human. For example, if you're creating a ten-minute performance about a local beach, what stories or perspectives would a flock of seagulls or a starfish share? How might the waves comment on a recent report by marine scientists? Ten minutes isn't very long: you could perform a handful of these suggestions as monologues, adding in elements of media, movement, and design, and you would already have an interesting piece.

Try and find a structure that ties everything together. Especially if your performance does not follow a single plotline with an inherent beginning, middle, and end, consider logical ways to sequence things. This could be geographical: if your team journeyed together from your rehearsal room to wherever your Subject is found, what might you discover on the way? Or your structure could be chronological – your story could start at dawn and move through midnight. You could begin in the distant past, and progress toward an imagined future. Whatever structure you decide on, write your discoveries into a shared script that everyone can follow and rehearse. Lastly, don't forget to give your piece a title that the Librarian can announce in Scene 9!

5. Put It All Together, and Answer the "Post-Devising" Prompts (60–64, 69–71, 81, 83–86).

After your devising work, it's time to weave the piece that you've created into the structure of the larger play. There's one last set of prompts to answer: the ones that reference your actual ten-minute performance and the process of creating it. This part is a kind of magic trick: you're showing your audience the seeds of ideas that will later grow into your full piece.

Start by revisiting the "Object Work" sequence in Scene 4. Think back to your own devising, and decide what the characters will explore and share at the beginning of this scene (prompts 60–64 and 69–71). Then look ahead to Scene 8, and think about how to stage the characters' onstage preparation in a way that reflects your own work – and gets all the needed elements of your own devised piece in place!

Once you've made those decisions, you're ready to put it all together. Take time to make sure that everyone is on the same page – literally! This is a great moment for your dramaturg/stage manager/assistant director to verify that everyone is now working with the same complete version of the play, including Miranda's script, your finalized answers to all the prompts, and the text of your devised ten-minute performance. Congratulations! At this point, you're ready to make final preparations and share your own unique version of this work.

In Closing

There are many ways to approach the creative challenges that this play offers. Don't stress about depicting every possible dimension of your subject: be realistic about the time you have, and focus on making something that brings you joy – something that you're genuinely excited to share. Check out the "Works" page on LubDub's website (lubdubtheatre.com) for examples of our performances and the ways that we devise.

Finally, be sure to celebrate your time together. We suggest cake.

– **Caitlin Nasema Cassidy, Robert Duffley,
Geoff Kanick, and Miranda Rose Hall**

PROMPT LIST

Scene One

1.

Scene Two

2.

Scene Three

3.

4.

5.

6.

7.

8.

9.

10.

11.

12.

13.

14.

15.

16.

17.

18.

19

20.

21.

22.

23.

24.

25.

26.

27.

28.

29.

30.

31.

31a.

32.

33.

    1.

    2.

    3.

34.

    4.

    5.

    6.

35.

    7.

    8.

    9

36.

    10.

    11.

    12.

13.

14.

15.

37.

38.

16.

39.

17.

18.

19.

40.

20.

41.

42.

43.

44.

45.

46.

47.

48.

49.

50.

51.

52.

52a.

53.

54.

55.
56.

57.

58.

59.

Scene Four

60.

61.

62.

63.

64.

64a.

65.

Scene Five

66.

67.

68.

69.

70.

71.

72.

Scene Seven

73.

74.

75.

76.

77.

78.

79.

80.

81.

82.

Scene Nine

83.

84.

85.

86.

87.

www.ingramcontent.com/pod-product-compliance
Lightning Source LLC
Chambersburg PA
CBHW070647120726
47909CB00004B/1614